The Wistful Wild

Fairy Tale Poems
of Longing and Ferocity

Edited by Stephanie Ascough

The Wistful Wild
February 2023.
Copyright © 2022 Stephanie Ascough, Stephanie Escobar, Caitlin Gemmell, Cortney Joseph, Jess Lynn, Beth Stedman.
ISBN: 978-1-7349812-3-0

Published by Stephanie Ascough.
Cover Art created by Stephanie Ascough.

Table of Contents

Dedication

For the ones always looking under layers of story

_____

Foreword

Compiling an anthology is much like preparing a spell. Elements must be gathered with care, selected in auspicious circumstances. The timing is often influenced by seasons of the earth and phases of the moon. Everything must then simmer before it is complete. She may not know exactly how long that will take, for this is no exact science, and she must watch her cauldron carefully. Left on the fire too long, the ingredients run the risk of turning bitter, curdling sour in uncertainty and self-doubt. Removed too soon, the brew will taste dull and shallow, lacking the desired depth of flavor required to bring about the desired result.

But the most important element is this: preparing the spell isn't a solitary undertaking.

The fairy tale witch is often pictured as a lone figure, an ugly old woman cackling wickedly over a boiling cauldron of poison. But long before men such as the Brothers Grimm gathered fairy tales from cooks and parlor maids and stamped their own name on them, people told each other stories as they worked. Over the fire, the needle, the vegetable plot. Stories were shared in groups, between generations.

In the writing down and retelling of these stories, elements changed and were added, removed, or replaced. Events and people deemed inappropriate or at odds with the dominant culture or religion were substituted with something more palatable. Intended audiences changed, too.

Seventeen years after Madame Villeneuve wrote *Beauty and the Beast* for adults, Madame le Prince de Beaumont wrote a moralized version for children. Centuries later, Disney incorporated beautiful, animated artwork and a signature sanitization into many stories, such as *Cinderella* and *Sleeping Beauty*.

Despite the practice of attaching one person's name to a vast collection of stories, narrative remains a collective experience. From the team of artists who create an animated film to the people who watch that film in their living room, fairy tales remain something we experience together. Even when we are reflecting on our individual experiences while interacting with a fairy tale, we're never totally disconnected from others.

Imagine a witch of indeterminate age, not bent and wrinkled (yet), peering over her cauldron and searching for the right ingredient. It comes to her like the proverbial bolt of lightning. What she needs is other people—witches, if you will—not so she can feed them to her pot, but so they can add their own ingredients and skill, maybe stir it, too. At her invitation, other herbalists and magic weavers emerge from their cottages, caves, and castles, bringing what only they can bring to the cauldron. The brew is infinitely richer than it ever would have been from the labors of one solitary woman. Each participant sees something a little different from her place around the fire—a glint of gold, a pearl of dew, a sprinkle of dust—and adds it to the pot.

There. You have the start of *The Wistful Wild*.

One day in the spring of 2021 I sat looking at a handful of fairy tale poems I'd written in a rare flurry of inspiration. (My muse is usually very slow.) I wanted to publish them. Should I write more and publish a book? Submit them to different publications? It occurred to me that it would be a much more fun and satisfying endeavor to share the experience and invite others to join me.

None of us live near one another, but our collective labors have brought us together. None of us qualify as crones when it comes to age, but we've drawn on generations of experience, the bitter and the sweet, the cautionary and the romantic.

There's been plenty of wicked cackling, too. We haven't made poison, but we certainly haven't shied away from the grittier, grimmer side of fairy tales, either. Our resources appeared centuries ago and during our own lifetimes. We've written about witches, yes, but also mermaids, stepsisters, fairies, princesses, and maids. Princes devious and devoted. Wolves, bears, sparrows, and swans.

Now, we step back from our cauldron and invite you to enjoy the fruits of our creative labors. They are homespun and passionate, more cottage industry than king's court. But don't mistake homespun for simple: these poems are rich, diverse, and complex. You just might find yourself returning for seconds.

Stephanie Ascough, editor and author

"Once Upon a Time" - Jess Lynn

Don't speak these words lightly.
Watch as you stir–
the cauldron boils,
not a drop may be lost!

Once we were wild women,
nothing escaped our hands, we
cradled babies and coaxed hearthfires,
even seeds sprouted by our blood.

Upon our breasts the
poets nursed and bones sang.
Onward, we followed the wheel
never thinking to hide our healing.

A traveler took our yarns, our words,
and bottled them in his pen,
wrapped and bound in parchment,
sold across the land.
We were subdued–nullified,
Or so they thought.

Time is on our side,
in that we were and always are
made with the warp and weft of stories,
expanding the thread between our hearts.

Stir, child, stir!

Now whisper the incantation
"Once upon a time",
for we have tales to spin.

On Becoming Briar Rose - Caitlin Gemmell

Tiptoe into the woods at dawn,
quietly so as not to vanish the magic.

Walk barefoot on the moss and pine
littered ground. Listen to the birdsong.
Do you hear blackbird, cuckoo,
and thrush?

Place bird seed in the palm of your hand
and offer it skyward. Stand so still you
fuse with the earth.

When a bird lands on your arm
speak to it softly –
make your voice a song.

And most importantly, know you don't
need mastery of a sword or a warrior's
aggression to be strong.

Kindness and a loving heart are the most
powerful magic of all and some women
were born to be doves.

Black Swan - Stephanie Escobar

O, poor Odette,
a most sorrowful portrait
a swan awaiting the moon;
beak downturned, ever demure,
the waters asparkle with noon.

Perhaps she's thinking of him, her prince
Dreaming up another escape from this;
Languishing in love's starvation —
She must think herself so hopeless,
so beyond salvation

When she does not know that she could be
far more damned –
                    she could be *me*

And O, Odette, if I could be you!
So tragic and doomed
yet free in your misery
You wear only fetters of feathers
and not the cold chains of jealousy.

There is nothing I would not do
to be just like you
I'd be your mirror image, the shadow of your wan,
your darker reflection,
your Black Swan.

By The Cinders - Cortney Joseph

I sit by the cinders,
Watching as life passes in phases,
Moving swiftly,
Leaving me in a constant daze.
Reminded with each strike of the clock,
I've nothing but my dreams
Of what never was, and what should've been,
And what has been in this life behind a lock.

I sit by the cinders,
Left with few friends of the unexpected kind,
Talking softly,
Holding tightly to what bit of joy I can find.
With my thoughts of love yet unseen,
With my ideas of the most charming,
Wide-eyed, pure, and everlasting love,
Waiting for the day it becomes more than a dream

12 Cinquains for 12 Dancing Princesses - Beth Stedman

at first
it was one night
a single decision
to stay up when everyone slept
to dance

but then
the next night came
and we didn't want to sleep
without keepers and watchers, we
were free

under
a full moon, we
twirled to a new rhythm
and discovered under the bed
a door

magic
that's what it was
a magic door that led
to a magic kingdom where we
could rule

there was
no one here to
tighten our corsets and
bind us, control us, and tell us

to sleep

we danced
with no limits
found twelve princes, each one
more handsome than the last
and eager

to please
kisses like dreams
dances where we could lead
spin the night, together or alone
we choose

twirl for
no one's eyes
but our own, no one ruled
another, with lectures and needs
just free

but always
it ended with
the rising of the sun
and we returned with worn shoes and
bruised hearts

they took
this from us, too
cheated us of freedom
found in the silence of the dark
magic night

we were
followed into
the safest place we'd known
stolen from the true princes who
loved us

our needs
discarded, our
wants replaced with nice shoes
tucked away under tight dresses
hidden

Three Rose Petals - Stephanie Ascough

Three questions unfurl,
Petals opening in a rose garden.
Who grew them in the first place?

Surely not the Beast,
All ferocious finery.
Rather a cavalcade of servants, invisible.

Secondly, surely her father was not the only person
Who could bring her one?
Was there no mother figure, grandmother, aunt,

Who could show Beauty
How to grow her own roses?

Thirdly, did she really have a choice?
We laud her bravery.
Do we question the actions,

Planted long ago, which backed her into a corner
As sharp as thorns?

Three questions expand.
As with all growing things,
Closer attention reveals further detail,

Like petals unfurling
In a rose garden.

Everywhere and Nowhere - Jess Lynn

I did not see this coming
How I knew you before
—in the dark
Pressed together for warmth
The way your voice lulled me to sleep
how your hand cupped my cheek
Fingers gliding through my hair
Breath whispered in my ear,
"Are you afraid?"

And in your eyes, the blue of winter skies,
I saw you as I met you, riding from my father's house
 "Are you afraid?"
No, not afraid, I answered,
digging my fingers into bristling fur. *Just cold.*
You nestled me in your coat whispering,
"Hold onto me, there's nothing to fear."

You are everywhere
and nowhere, my love.
The distance between us
blooms like a compass rose.

In the dark, legs caress
under silken sheets
Your bearskin shed for a night's sleep
But I knew you,
by the beat of your breath
And when I asked to see your face,
your mouth cried, "You must never."

But in the depth of your sigh,
I heard your reply, a desperate
longing to be known as a
man and not a beast.

But I could not tell my heart
to wait, though I knew you
with nothing to fear.
The lamp held high,
three drops and
your awakened cry.

Oh, if only I waited in sullen hibernation,
my love, what have I done?

At dawn your pad feet hit the floor,
the wet snout teased me by day
and the nose nuzzled me at night.
But now I am frigid without you by my side.
I cannot go with you, but I will follow
You are east of the sun and west of the moon

The crone's cry,
"Perhaps you are the one destined
to unwind the spell?
You'll get there too late or never."
Late or never, late or never,
rings in return.

How can I answer?
What must be my reply?
To the east–

I climbed on the back of the wind,
"Never flown that far,
But if you will, I'll go with you"
It held not a drop of your warmth
No fur to nestle in, no hand to protect me

Not afraid, I said, and closed my eyes.

To the west—
I rode along the wind,
"Never flown that far,
But if you will, I'll go with you"
Scrambling, I held to its rumbling
No quiet timbre or gentle smile

Not afraid, I said, and lowered my head.

To the south—
I held to the wind,
"Never flown that far,
But if you will, I'll go with you"
Blustered about, blowing
How you'd hate the squandered time

Not afraid, I said, and sighed.

To the north—
I clung to the wind,
"Never flown that far,
But if you will, I'll go with you"
And chaos followed in its wake

No comfort in its exasperated arms.

Not afraid, I said, and prayed.

You are the heart of my compass
the north star guiding me and
the southern wind at my back
You are the dawn of my right hand
And the sun that carries me home

I will find you, my love, for you
you are everywhere and nowhere
All at once

Kaguya-Hime - Stephanie Escobar

Too much is the earth
that I beg for the moon's
numb, pale company.
Swathed in the lightest
silk I'm still too weighed
by this gravity.

Emperor, write me no more!
Your bride I cannot be.
Not all the gold of this earth,
nor the bronze promises of man,
can keep me.

Mother, Father,
will you understand when I leave?
Ascend again to my celestial home,
leaving you alone, in your old age, to grieve?

My entourage is coming—soon I will forget!
Every name and face to slip away,
yet my heart—my heart may always feel the iron weight
of worldly regret.

The One in Which the Princess Marries Her Best Friend - Caitlin Gemmell

Your prince isn't always the gilded hero you've known five minutes
before deciding he's the one.
This flagrant braggart, smooth talking dreamboat,
the popular one with a winning smile
and false promises between his plastic teeth.
Instead, what if your prince is your loyal friend,
stalwart companion in the wild wood
where your murmuring willow voice
revealed all the secrets of your soul
and his bass note lips
promised eternal friendship.
This prince's character unfurls
petal by petal, softly, painstakingly slowly,
Taurean patience a blessing
and a curse.
He's the friend who held you
in your darkest moments,
gave wings to your wishes
and let you fly away towards your own idea of heaven.
His bruised heart loved you silently,
waited twenty years for your return
when your wings could no longer breathe air
and needed to be
submerged in water
to function as they were always meant,
for you to realize
he was the true hero of your story all along.

Rhiannon (The Lady of Yesterday) - Jess Lynn

You seek wonder upon the mound
Watching as I ride, encircling to track
Who is the hunt and who is the hunter?

Your men, they cannot catch me
Your fastest steed will not reach me
Though I trot, I pass you by.

Your might will not draw me
You cannot follow, nor match my speed
I am a maiden you cannot catch.

"For the sake of him who you love best
stay for me," your voice carries.
Love?—Yet you know me not.

You speak of love
Isn't it presumptuous to assume
That means you?

Am I not a mere vision before you?
A picture of your longing unfurled?
A banner to carry, a prize to be won?

Come closer Pwyll, King of Dyfed
I am Rhiannon, daughter of Hefeydd the Old,
Your Lady of Yesterday.

Three days you watched,
Before you came yourself,
Before you moved to claim me.

Ask and you shall receive,
Seek and I will flee
Is this a game? Why, yes, I too can play.

I am my own woman,
My own errand,
"No husband will I have but my love for you."

One year's time
The wedding feast laid
You I placed in the stead of him I loathed

Your generosity at an unknown's request
He nearly bested you, I held my tongue
And waited, again, one year's time

I took my fate from man's hands
and you, dear Pwyll,
nearly ruined it.

Tossed across the chessboard of Cymru*
When I only wanted to be me--
The trickery I must resort to

To be my own person
To hold my own name

To take my own counsel

I am your Lady of Yesterday.

*Wales

Haiku of a Red Hooded Girl - Beth Stedman

In the deep forest
I noticed you and hungered,
Desiring your bite

Red and the Wolf - Caitlin Gemmell

It wasn't the wolf who devoured Red.
She went looking for his wild masculinity,
each step a siren's song, luring him to his death.

You thought her basket contained food for Granny
instead of a pin-pricked heart and a perfume
trailing seduction.

She ripped him open and fed his bones
to the wishing well where he was reborn –
a man of her own design.

Maleficent's Lament - Cortney Joseph

My eyes hold the color of envy,
My heart, hardened like thorns waiting to prick
Any and all who dare seek to trespass on land forbidden,
Where I've been hidden, banished.
Left to wither away like wilted rose petals.
My lips stained the shade of ash,
My mind, holding long jaded views
Of a world bent on destroying a heart,
That'd already been torn apart, broken.
Left to rest in pieces strewn about carelessly.
My skin, pale as their sleeping beauty's,
My trust, broken by the betrayal of a pompous fool
Scurrying and scrambling to beg my forgiveness,
Now seeking my presence, pleading,
Left to feel as if it were I who were in the wrong.
When all I'd wanted, like most humans and creatures alike,
was
To be loved.

Vigil - Stephanie Escobar

Gauze of tattered spider's silk
clothe the castle like a cocoon
the sovereigns slumber forevermore
within this dust-piled tomb

The courtiers poised still to dine
heaving rhythmic snores
causing cobwebs to quiver
with their breathy roars

And the golden princess
who should be dead
instead beads drool on her pillow
and turns her pretty head

A prize of glory, surely
for a brave prince to take—
surpass the cursed forest
and a lovely princess wake

The princes, how they try
to slash through my thorns
with armored steeds
and flashing swords

Though always they're greeted
by my fiery hiss
for no prince shall ever live

to deliver True Love's Kiss

Three Women - Stephanie Ascough

Maleen

Seven years I wait, dark and silent as a tomb
My escape leaves me naked as a child from the womb

I find the one my heart desires, but he believes my death
Has tied him to another who would steal my very breath

She binds me in her wedding clothes, a silencing death
shroud
Will I let this be my end, my own freedom disavowed?

Silent I cannot remain, when all these years I've fought
to live as I see fit and good and not as I've been taught

I lift my voice and scream aloud, rending this deception,
I free myself, I free my love, we claim our shared affection.

Maid

Chosen for this thankless task, I attest refusal's price:
The judgment for defiant daughters is rigid and precise.

I thought perhaps that in the dark we shared a sympathy
Consolation, broken bread, erasing lines of pedigree.

Yet when we broke into the world,
And freedom like a leaf uncurled,

You were content to go your way and simply let me fade.
Your story carried on. Who am I but just a maid?

Now I am left forgotten, past devotion cast aside.
I must find another story. This one, I will decide.

Princess

Girls born without the fortune of required beauty or sweet charm
Must claw their mark upon a world resolved to cause them harm.

Her grace and goodness posed a threat disastrous to my life
I had won this prince myself; I must make myself his wife.

Her beauty I would borrow, her lovely voice I stole
Do you think me brutal? Wicked? Do you think I have no soul?

My soul and body paid the price of death humiliating.
For beauty always wins, charm's rules undeviating.

I suppose I have myself to blame, bitter, full of hate,
For a world always consigning ugly girls to ugly fates.

Mirror, Mirror - Cortney Joseph

Vanity had never been becoming for a woman,
But it was all I'd known, it was all-consuming.
I looked forward to daily viewings of my perfection,
Looked forward to being showered in adoration,
The object of great admiration. It was routine, set with
intention,
Met with expectation of nothing less than the truth.
It was I, the fairest of them all.
In beauty, in grace, in my actions, in my ruling of the lands.
It was I, the most deserving
Of the accolades, of the fawning,
Of nobles and subjects falling to their feet at the mere sight
of me.
It was I, the Queen.
And when I stepped forward, I awaited my reward.
"Mirror, Mirror on the wall,
Who is the fairest one of all."

In my vanity, I smiled, adjusted the crown
That rested comfortably atop the throne it belonged.
It was obvious, and it'd never been wrong.
"It's been you, My Queen, always. But today, I must say…"
I looked on with caution, wondering what could be so
important
That it must come before my deserved adulation.
"In a land nearby, hidden in the cottage of seven dwarfs,
Dwells a great beauty fairer than thee."
And before me the glass cracked, leaving me no way to ask
From where this sudden blasphemy had come.
It IS I, the Queen, and shall REMAIN I, the Queen.
Of that I'll make sure, if I must go to the ends of the world

To rid these lands of any who'd have the gall
To present themselves as fairer than me.

Snow Eats an Apple - Caitlin Gemmell

Perfect, unblemished red.
Pink-tinged flesh tingles
her tongue. More whore
than virgin, enchantress
instead of princess. Whispers,
"You can be powerful too."

Snow was cunning, brave.
Snow craved, craved,
craved the witch's power.
Which is why she bit
into the poisoned apple,

sunk into the underworld
where she discovered

          all the secrets
          of the universe.

Hunger - Stephanie Escobar

the breadcrumbs we scatter
blend with the pine needles and leaves
Father's shoes crunch
upon,
as he brings us
      yet again
           into the forest.

Brother and I
slung like piglets over his
shoulders,
we watch how the
crows fly down and peck
our desperate trail.

the sight of bread in their beaks
makes my stomach scream!
how long has it been since I've chewed?
tasted?
if only I could be a crow and fly.

dropped upon the ground—
bashed upon the head—
we wake in the gloaming dark woods
unknowing west from east
or up
      from down
and we think, at last, it will happen!
surely by dawn we will sleep
forever

unless, already, it's happened . . .
already heaven is here!
for not far of our
tripping and stumbling in the dark
lies a
rainbow-house,
          bright in the night

a cottage of colorful confection

my mouth floods
and Brother runs!
          no hesitation to lick
                    the candy walls
suckle the door—chew the gingerbread
eaves

but I stand back,
          a little fearful—
                    for an eerie sense
suggests that, perhaps
this is not heaven
at all,
but the Devil's sweet temptation
to hell

and Brother!
oh, Brother is so greedy . . .

we are both so hungry
that even the smell of an oven
baking foul meat smells sweet

"Oh, my!"
comes a voice
like the Devil himself
     dressed in syrup

the door opens to an old woman,
fattened by too many meats

   "Sweet little children!
    You must be so hungry."

and we are

Bluebeard - Beth Stedman

The man my sister married wore a sunny smile
a disposition that burned, bright and hot

I didn't like him but what could I say?

He had a way of bringing people into orbit
and my sister was just the sort of planet
he wanted
beautiful and admired
a shining star that lit the sky on fire

On the day of their wedding, she smiled
while I sewed my lips shut
and toasted
    to the bride

Year one:
a child

Year two:
another—
to fix what she thought only just broke

Year three:
a councilor telling her
    he's the sun
    the center

a burning fire holding all the power
Be a good wife
Things will change

Year four:
another child
and her light dimmed

Year five:
a bruise on the cheek
an accident

Year six:
a trap
a tower
a warning
    Don't open locked doors
    Don't ask questions
Become like the night
Empty and afraid

Like a shooting star
She finally tried to escape

Too late.

Snow White - Beth Stedman

Did Snow White really sing
while she cleaned seven men's underwear,
cooked seven men a feast every night,
slept with seven blankets
tucked up to her chin?

Did she remind herself
seventy-seven times each day
this was better than death?

Did she run to greet them
at seven o'clock each evening?
Or did she quiver when she heard
the footsteps
   of seven men
     coming
       close
         voices raised
           in rivalry

Did she want to run seven thousand miles away?
And take her chances among the trees?

I have a hard time believing
a woman
alone
wouldn't be afraid
in a situation like that
with a history like hers

in a world like ours.

Rumpelstiltskin's Daughter - Jess Lynn

My father was a small man
Painted the color of greed
—but never green.

His name a secret whispered
Over hearth fires,
Spoken only when necessary
By those truly desperate

He gave what they desired,
and then some
And yet it was he—not them,
Painted as vindictive, greedy, soulless

But—
Was it he who sold his daughter to the highest bidder?
Was it he who said straw could become gold?
        What strange alchemy!
Was it he who threatened death if there was none by morn?
Was it he who kept his bride locked until his coffers were
filled?
Was it he who bargained their first born?
Was it he who forgot such a bargain?

No.

I'd rather not grow up
in such a household,

among such people
willing to lie & toss aside

And so,
I took that small man's hand and
left my gilded birth.
For now I am
Rumpelstiltskin's daughter.

Hand-me-downs - Stephanie Ascough

My mother hands me a knife.
I know what it is for.
I must carve my own foot,
make myself smaller,
fit for a prince,
a man who does not even see my face.

My sister was handed the same fate,
yet all the good it did her.
She whimpers, sits in the corner like
a discarded sock, bloodied
with yesterday's choices,
grand aspirations ebbing away
in a scarlet tide.
She begs me not to do it.

But what else is there?
Will the knife slice by another's hand,
if not by mine?
What else is there to do
but wonder:
Mother,
who handed you the knife first?

Kitchen Magic - Stephanie Ascough

Sweep the ashes, scrub the floors,
collect kindling dry as stale dreams.
I weep, and rain kisses the grave.

Boil the water, cook their food,
I swallow crumbs
and leavings by firelight.

Mend the clothes, brush the shoes,
I glean gossip and news:
a festival of luxury and matrimony is coming.

Tend the garden, visit the grave,
speak loving memories.
I wish, I wish, I wish.

Comb her hair, stitch this hem,
No, Cinderella, if you went out in this rain,
you'd melt into ash!

They fret and worry,
the rain will surely
spoil the king's festival.

The birds have all flown away
and I am damp with soot and sorrow.
I weep, I weep, I weep.

Coal black night, a knock on wood
I scramble to see—
An old woman, perhaps, or a vagabond.

She is young as I, and forgotten, too,
and terrors haunt her eyes,
some I cannot understand.

She enters gratefully, wearily,
her cloak a patchwork of furs.
I share my sparse bread, and she, her sharp stories.

We sleep in soot, but
the night has stopped weeping,
and I dream of a garden of gold.

Morning dawns bright.
My companion cooks, simmers soup,
and my burden is lighter.

The kitchen is a merry kingdom:
friendship, shared burdens, even laughter.
Can a stranger be a sister?

Lace these corsets, paint these faces,
Cinderella, your smile is unbecoming!
At least your cooking's improved.

Carriage wheels rattle.
We watch them go and smile.

The house exhales, and so do we.

Two pigeons alight on the windowsill,
and a fresh breeze fills the kitchen.
I hear singing above the grave.

Has the weather changed, or have I?
we finish work, we two sister-companions,
while festivals fade to dusty glass.

This room of soot and scraps,
of alchemy and quiet work,
witnesses the real treasure of our own making.

We have begun something brilliant.
It fills the kitchen, spills out into the garden, and
we dream, we scheme, we brew.

Belle's Delicious Library - Caitlin Gemmell

What if you could visit Belle's library
and it's run by an eagle-eyed librarian
and instead of asking for a book by its title
you say, "I'd like chocolate mousse
with pecans and whipped cream,"
or "salmon fricassee
with grilled artichokes and butter, please,"
or "Today? Lemon violet cream."
What would you order? And when the librarian
offers you books to fit your cravings,
what if with every bite you read
your hunger is satiated, soul satisfied.
That's my idea of paradise.

Tink's Discovery - Cortney Joseph

Hidden in the mist, she watched with glee
As a figure in green meandered a short distance away
A sight unusual, much larger than she,
A child it seemed in search of a place most safe

She moved with caution from petal to petal
Her sparkly trail settling ever so softly,
For interacting with a human would surely be monumental
But moving with haste, the effect could surely be costly

Without warning excitement overtook her,
Her light sparking in little spurts and flickers
A powerful glow giving away where she hovered
Growing in intensity with each second she lingered

Silently panicking, she fought to gain control of her tears
Her curiosity, it seemed, had gotten the best,
And scaring away the boy was now her greatest fear
The moment could end in one big mess.

Within a matter of seconds, her cover was blown
He stood, astonished by her diminutive size,
Glad that, suddenly, he was no longer alone
She, intrigued by his mischievous grin and bright brown
eyes

His playful voice spoke out, curiosity unbound,
Sprite, Fairy, a little twinkle of dust?

"Well, what are you? What kind of new friend have I
found?"
Whatever she was, he felt at ease, he could trust

"We can have a ton of fun! No need to be afraid of me."
She circled him once, assessing the boy
He continued confidently, "Just wait, you'll see!"
A game, he figured, he played along with joy

He giggled and ran, she chased and followed
Leaves rustling beneath his feet, he paused only briefly to
think
As they played all through the world of Pixie Hollow
The wondrous sounds her trailing made, "I'll call you Tink!"

And friends they'd be from that day forward,
A lost boy and a little woodland fairy.
No danger, no troubles, not a soul he'd let harm her.
For one another, a great love, they would always carry.

Beauty - Stephanie Ascough

Tell me all your secrets.
I'll stay and wind them
About my hands,
Embrace them
in my soul,
Keep them safe in
The very shadows of
my being.

Show me all your fears.
I'll drown them
in my laughter
And release them at
the first stroke of the new moon,
Spinning them back into
joy
burning
in our blood.

Beast - Stephanie Ascough

Already my fears are fleeing
at the touch of your hand.
But as for secrets,
What are yours?
I want to know
the scent of all
your secret dreams
the sound of all
your hidden desires
the taste of all
your deepest longings.

Open yourself to me
the way you've opened me
to your heart.

Cloak of Invisibility - Caitlin Gemmell

My path to the castle paused
at a crossroads where my story
joined a wise crone, princess in disguise.
Her captivating eyes
entranced me.
Willingly, I accepted the cloak of invisibility,
signed the contract with the breath of my life.

Enlisted to ferret out their secret
were princes trapped in a strange dream existence,
for her sisters' hearts were cold, unlike her own.
She only wanted an escape from the reality
of their life of royal duty,

Conjured a doorway leading to the place
where they could shed their swan cloaks
and waltz freely.

It was her sisters who held the princes spellbound.
She wished to follow the thread around to the
beginning, release them from their burial mound.

Her beguiling eyes knit me
into a pattern as yet unknown.
As I was already following my thread to the castle
her scheme was my lantern
guiding me to the center of the labyrinth.

That night, I followed the princesses through
their secret doorway into a bejeweled forest
almost as exquisite as my princess's wild soul.

The twig I snapped from a golden tree,
proof of the enchantment they did weave,
was tucked into a fold of my invisibility cloak.
Next morning I couldn't bear to offer it to the king
for it would mean
their secret was exposed and I would see the
princess no more.
Anger flashed in her eyes
When she realized
I had not yet spoken my truth.
But I told her the king would need more proof
And she reluctantly agreed this was wise.

That night, a silver twig found its way to my
invisibility cloak. Instead of dancing, my princess
hovered in the shadows, whispering secrets.
Sunlight flooded my soul
As we shared our stories.
Pain cut through my heart as the realization
Pierced me, tomorrow would be the last time
I could gaze into her cunning grey eyes.

Next morning she asked why I had not yet
Revealed their secret to the king.
I spoke of needing proof but we both knew
This was a lie.
I was trying to slow time
So threads would dance between us
A fraction longer.

Through the doorway to the enchanted wood
We emerged a third time, my hand in the princess's
As if our lives depended on their union.
Throwing caution to the winds, we danced together
Our threads braiding into an eternal knot.

My cloak slid off, the masquerade ending,
Ushering in a new beginning
So long as I passed the test
Her eleven sisters now set me.
I was invited to dine
On velvet luxuriousness
And somehow I knew to avoid the wine.

Pretending to take a sip, the princess tipped
The goblet away from my lips
Spilling our path to freedom.
The sound of magic shattering
Caused a tumultuous reaction
And we all dashed into a new chapter.

A third twig, diamond lighted, was added to
The clues I offered the King.
Overjoyed to see kindness in his daughters' eyes
The king offered me any prize
My heart desired.
I glanced at my princess and saw her heart
Still sang in harmony with mine.
The king agreed we could wed
And to this day my love refuses to shed
Light on the mystery of the origins of the
Cloak of invisibility.

Some days my wife is more crone than princess
And I love her in every aspect
Of her becoming.

VALEMON - Stephanie Escobar

I know you only by night
by silhouettes and scents
within the velvet veil of shadow
Blindly grasping in the dark
the feel of your flesh
                  human flesh
the contours of your back,
                 lithe and smooth
Your strength grasped within my arms.
Though haunted I am
by flashes of day-
             of the bright winter sky
       and white fur

I know you not by day
though so clearly I see you
lumbering through sleeping orchards
     heavy paws crunching snow
my king of claws and teeth.
So clearly I see you
yet desperately I await the dark again
     for man again
Shrouded in shadow
face forbidden
     even to me

I know you hardly at all
yet your children I've swelled with
              birthed
and in their small faces I've sought yours.

But as evanescent as their father
                  they disappear
one, by one
                  lost to me

I know only the fleeting snow
for I am the wife of shadows
        the mother of memories
Impatient,
I grip the candle;
After all these years,
the tallow light begs to find your face
        against all consequence
        for have we not suffered enough?

Do I dare to know you by light?

Rapunzel's Rhapsody - Cortney Joseph

Resting on the sill of a window,
At the top of the highest tower,
Covered in wild vines,
Picking at the petals
Of dried sunflowers.
Hidden away in a forest,
Furthest from a world I recall
Only in memories, in dreams,
Wishing and waiting
For comfort found in company.

The coils of my hair
Falling and resting in ways most natural,
Called for the attention of my gentle hands,
To be brushed from end to root,
With the same care and love
I have longed for, yearned for.
To be tucked away in protection,
While I wish to be found,
Swept away into the world,
And a life worth living

I've waited with patience as strong
And infinite as the styles I've tried,
Braided and twisted,
Curled, loc'd, and straightened strands
The length of this sentence
Of solitude I've served.
When's my turn, I wonder
Fancying my hair a tendril-like ladder,

Hoping it'd be with ease I could climb down
Touch the ground, and finally ... run.

Ropes and Reins - Stephanie Escobar

I bundle armfuls of my hair and
dump it out the tower window—
Watch it slither and thump with
glossy weight.

He takes handfuls and hoists himself
up, up, up,
hand over hand over hand,
his dead weight hanging

And I blink away the tears
that burn in my eyes,
my scalp nearly tearing.
My face scrunches—holding back
a cry.
Head lolling, neck straining,
hands bracing the ledge.

And what does he do
when he comes through?
Before I can wipe my eyes, he
lays heavy kisses to my unreceiving mouth.
And his hands slide
up to my scalp,
where he tugs at my hair

  again.

Rapunzel's True Story - Caitlin Gemmell

They came in the night with their bright torches
and bitter hatred, raucous voices bellowing,
"Burn the witches."

My wise teacher, protector, mother urged me
take your twins and flee. But how could I leave
her to be blackened to ash?

I took her brittle hand in mine as if our flesh
could be fused together, chanted magic words
never taught to me, just known intimately

For as I'd grown from maiden to mother
spells came to me so effortlessly,
pupil now equal to teacher.

My witch mother who gave me a home,
taught me how to peer into the mirror of humanity,
see each person's story, a map only decipherable
to witches

shook her head, trapped animal eyes telling me
two witches would not be enough to defeat
a hundred men with their knives and flames.

I saw his face in the crowd, the prince who stole

my body. For the first time, icy fear gripped me
until the frantic heartbeats of my children

melted this fear and rage overcame me
I wondered, did he care he was about
to murder his own children?

Once more my mother urged me to escape.
"Think of your children," she said, and I was proud
to see her eyes held no fear.

She stood calmly, regally. I nodded as tears pooled
onto the ground. She cut my hair with her athame
one quick slice and it was done.

With my children on my back I climbed down the rope
of golden hair and walked away from the tower that
kept me safe from witch hunters until now.

I became a forest wife, living in trees and abandoned huts
subsisting on rabbits, mushrooms, and stories,
my children far too scrawny but wondrously alive.

Songs came back to me inch by inch, miraculously.
I never intended for my song to be a love spell
but the magic unfolded anyway.

A ribbon of red drew him close to me.
He had a crow on his shoulder
and goodness in his eyes. Tattoos covered his arms;

his own magic much like my spells were mine.

My forest prince knew the language of birds and
thanked me for teaching him my witch songs.
He offered me a place beside him and I gladly

returned to his castle with him where I ruled
alongside him as queen but also witch who shared
my mother's potions and remedies widely.

The Princess & The Cobbler - Cortney Joseph

I watched him intently,
Searching for any sign that he, like I,
Felt the spark of something wonderful igniting.
His eyes held a nervousness,
A fear I wished to ward away with reassurance
That I, like he, wished for more than simple friendship.
I asked his name, smiling as he spoke lowly,
His gentle voice dancing around my mind,
Implanting itself like a beautiful melody I'll love for life.
"I'm just a cobbler, my name is of no importance, Princess."
I inched closer to him,
Watching the way he twiddled his thumbs, his eyes low,
Before returning his focus to the work he'd been given,
A simple task I created,
With the hopes of keeping him near to me,
With the hopes of growing closer, endearing myself to him.
"No formalities," I offered. "You can call me Yum-Yum, and
I shall call you?"
I almost missed it,
The softness of his voice barely carrying above the
pounding of our hearts,
Racing, I know, to join one another in love.
"Tack, is that it?"
It was unique, like he, a perfect fit for a cobbler so great
And on he continued, sewing a heart to close the torn
leather of my shoe,
A beautiful symbol of love I hoped we'd someday share

On The Surface - Cortney Joseph

From atop a rock, she rested,
Lazily skipping pebbles across the surface
Wondering which would touch the land first,
And if she'd ever get her chance too.

The sun shone brightly, warming her bronzed cheeks,
Slowly drying the scales of her fin,
Though she seemed not to mind,
Lost in her thoughts of excitement in a world anew.

Her friends watched with great concern,
Her sighs growing deeper, eagerness dancing in her eyes
Her sense of danger fleeting fast
As the thing they feared greatly came into view,

"You're already where you belong," they shouted to no
avail,
She'd jumped into the icy waters, moving swiftly,
Her destiny calling, her happiness awaiting
Their pleas ignored, nothing more they could do

With caution she slowed, pausing beside the keel
She could hear the celebration above,
A glorious array of voices and lively music,
Her excitement growing at the sight of 'sky fire'; white, red,
and blue

With great maneuvering, she hoisted herself high enough to
see
Peering inside the porthole, enamored at the sight before
her,
Enthralled by figures in wondrous garments, moving in
joyous motion
And there he stood, a prince among his crew.

She'd seen him before, a figure resting beneath the sea
In more than her dreams, his face she'd touched,
Lips she'd kissed, hand she'd held, body she'd pressed
against
Heart she'd captured, and all the while he had no clue

She watched intently, longing to be closer
Wishing she could move on two, could spin in circles
Laughing heartily until she found herself within his arms
again,
Held with certainty, showered with kisses, given a love so
true

"Your father will have a fit," a stern warning came from
below,
To which she peered and smiled, no fear stirred within
But she allowed herself to fall back into the hidden abyss,
Her mood, now, like that of the world below, cold and blue.

To dream of it was easy, whimsical explorations done in fun
A secret all hers, stolen moments most treasured
And they'd have to remain just that, a mermaid and her
fancies
For life on the surface, she could never pursue.

The Mermaid's Sacrifice - Beth Stedman

I gave up the ocean for the freedom to
stand on my own two feet
the cost didn't seem too high
my voice
for a dream
I thought love was enough
without words
I stood on the sand of a lie
                I would be loved more
                        silent

I didn't know my voice
Was its own kind of legs
A foundation
That roared with the force
Of the ocean
That carried me forward
And gave me
The power to
Run free

Displaced Mermaid - Caitlin Gemmell

Where are my mother's pearls?
And where is her strand of sea coral,

fractured when my two-legged husband
thrust it against the wall of our marital prison?

Where is my shadow, sea-finned
ephemeral reminder of the time before

I traded gills for lungs, underwater
autonomy for earthly durance vile?

Where is my image in the river?
She echoes the truth to me,

that no matter the shape my body
takes, I still yearn to breathe in the sea.

Bayou Blues - Cortney Joseph

The sounds of horns and strings, percussion and brass
Melted and blended into a melodious gumbo of Jazz
Bodies of all design, both lithe and writhing, joy amassed
As a second line passed beneath the wrought iron and
canopy
Of the balcony where a restless soul clung for comfort
Sweat dripped freely down mocha tinted skin,
Clinging to dainty fingertips that longed to caress the face
Of a newly lost friend, of a newly found love

For days on end, their time was all she seemed to recall.

It was a mystical force that bound them together,
A wayward prince who deemed his tricks most clever
That thought he would get through life with his looks
forever,
And a prideful girl of meager means, working her way
through Bourbon
Trying to fulfill her dreams with tasteful delicacies and food
she adored
A chance encounter born from jealousy and greed,
A grand mishap shifting the shape of bodies and lives of
two strangers
entangled in vengeful webs spun through incantations and
spells

What had been a test of patience, will, and wits,
Seemed to bring them both a round of life's most precious
gifts
Things that weren't defined by trappings, glamor, or glitz

Contentment that could only be found when two were still, relaxed
Living each moment as if it were the last, at peace with new surroundings
Away from madness of chasing money and overworking towards goals
Stuck in amphibious bodies until lessons were learned,
Unsure if they'd want to let go when they and life were normal again

And for days on end, then, it seemed the old life held nothing she'd want or need

Tearstained makeup voiding the mask of false smiles
Of giggles, of deep breaths in hopes of keeping up lies
In hopes of keeping *those* feelings locked and buried deep inside
A desire, it seemed, refusing to sleep like the city that held her wishes
kept all her dreams, where now she was destined to languish
Bright lights and high energy did nothing to ease the pain
Offered no relief to the broken heart, nothing to distract from the grief
Rising like the waters of the bayous 'til they overflowed

She could have one or the other, or nothing at all
And knowing this did nothing to soften the blow of the dangerous fall,
Had not stopped her from pressing forward and letting down guarded walls
From reveling in the peace, basking in the happiness within his company

She leapt forward, holding tightly until the lilies floated
from beneath her feet
Left her colorful skies a bleak gray, a heart broken into
pieces
As her prince bid a sorrowful goodbye, piercing like the
bellowing
Of a mournful blues tune down St. Charles Avenue

Jorinde - Beth Stedman

Once, a mother crone gave me feathered wings
to fly above elms and ash and spruce
above ambitious men and wooden towns
she thought she gave me freedom by taking
my love

She didn't know how my captured heart soared
with every look and touch and sweet, sweet kiss
of lips that spoke kind words against my skin
so she made me a bird and took me from
my love

Now, my broken heart flies from branch to branch
searching homes and fallow fields and green glens
always looking for my one and only
mourning every morning I wake without
my love

The Bird Witch - Beth Stedman

I built my home deep in the forest's heart
where blackbirds make their nests among the spruce
and cedar touches clouds high above any man

I built my home where I could dream of flight
where magic filtered through leaves of emerald green
and women found me when they wanted to leave

I made them birds who could soar into the blue
where crushing constraints were left behind
and they could make their homes as they please

I made them birds who could sing
where the sunlight meets the morning dew
and all who heard their song sang too

The Hoop Around My Heart - Jess Lynn

The hoop around my heart
Iron rivulets fastened tight
One curse broken and I, your bride
But it's Iron Henry at your side

You sit with your hand in his
And I, with this hoop around my heart
I did not ask for this---
To be bought and pried

Would I've let that golden ball
sink   sink   sink
to have lost such treasure is nothing
to these iron fetters

Iron sharpens iron, I see
He saved you by bringing you to me
And I, a pawn in your plan
Pressed upon by niceties

Why did no one question--
There was no refrain--
An amphibian by my plate
At my breast while I slept

Yes, I threw you against the wall
Does that make me ungrateful?
If all you needed was a hard throw,

Then why not ask me at the well?

Why must I be your bride?
My future now tied inexorably to yours
Is it pleasure to marry a stranger?
Forgotten as soon as the carriage door closed

Oh, I see--
his tears at your coming
Your hand in his
I am the hoop that keeps you bound to him
Now you may have your freedom, your love
And I? Oh, I have a hoop around my heart.

Firebird - Stephanie Escobar

Midnight orchard
      glowing gold
a mist of magic
weaving spells over sleepy eyes
but I catch a fiery glimpse
      just before the kiss of a dream
of wings aflame
a bird like the burning sun
greedy for gilt apples that crunch
      between beak and twig

      is this not a dream?

I lunge for the creature
capturing her flames in my arms
without burns to scar me
only brilliant light
searing my eyes to tears

      it must be a dream!

she flies out of my grasp
the sun to return to the sky
and I am left with only
a fragment of the fire

      a feather

burning flames still by day
and igniting my Father's greed

so it was no dream!

Speak, Reply - Jess Lynn

You scoff at fairy tales
Roll your eyes,
"They always have a happy ending."

Your cynicism reeks,
warts and all.

We did not know
that
when we set
out
how our tales would
end

You did not witness
the tears and bruises
between *"Once upon a time..."* and
        "Now some time had passed."

You call it happy–
to scrub the floors of your home
and be spat on,
To run from a
father's incestuous grip,
To be hunted & found,
To be buried alive,
swallowed whole,
To endure the loneliness and dust of
A hundred years' sleep

With only your thoughts
for company,
To discover the bloody corpse
of your predecessor,
To live sealed in a tower and when love came,
he left with his eyes gouged out.

The fairy tale's not so happy, is it?

Do you care to know
the scars woven
from our hands to
The fabric of our souls?

Yes, yes,
We have found our peace
Our happy end
But the damage
has been done,
Seeped into our bones
not so easily resolved

There are traumas,
scars between
> *"Once upon a time"*

and
> *"they lived happily ever after"*

that you will never see.
Night sweats and flashbacks,
places we can no longer bear to be,
how breath flees at the sound of a name.

But–yes,
Happily ever after, et al.

RE: Fairy tales have happy endings

A happy ending--
for who?
Oh...
justice?
Is that what this is?

Spitting frogs,
Eyes clawed out.
Bloodied feet,
Burned alive.

Are we beyond
redemption?
Can even wicked stepsisters
and evil queens
have holes in their hearts
and long for something more?

Turned
and tortured
to secure a place
in a world never meant
for us

So, cynic, we ask again,
A happy ending for who?

Stitching - Stephanie Ascough

Terrors haunt me,
Memories claw me,
Tease the silver filaments of trust
That used to guard my heart
But now hang like skinned creatures,
A disjointed thing quivering
In my chest.

Now I wear skins of another
Sort of creature,
A kinder embrace
And a kind of death,
Stitched with trembling fingers,
A patchwork I must wear
Over my shredded self.

Indeed, I make myself anew
As I wander
Far from the grasping,
The tearing, the thing
That never should have been
Yet was.

I make my bed in nettles,
Under trees,
Become
A creature of the woods.
No one's daughter,
No one's princess,
No one's possession.

A bag of gowns hides next to my skin,
A kernel of who I was,
My only just in case.
I begin to find pieces of myself
Between the roots and earth,
And sometimes,
Those pieces frighten me.

But onwards I journey.
From what do I run?
Myself or my past?
Both,
Stained with the shame and the crime
And the silent cry.
Both,
I think,
Or sometimes I do.
Sometimes forgetting is a gift
And others,
A trap.
I will not be caught again.

Weary, I see a spire piercing the sky,
A castle turret.
Having traveled so far,
I am too tired to run
Though this sight strikes terror anew
In my blood.
Yet this time,
My coat protects me.
This I tell myself as they take me in
And I am met with the greatest shock of all:
Welcome.

Days pass.
My coat collects the smells of the kitchen,
Smoke and salmon roasted,
Grease and gooseberry pie,
Soap and seasonings, spices.
No one wants to touch a haggard, furry creature,
Though they smile, most of them,
And let me work,
With them yet alone,
forming feasts for royalty.
Flour and fat and fillings are my needle and thread.
Am I making cakes or remaking myself?

Then in the courtyard
I see him,
A plain man, gently smiling,
As uncourtly as an everyday coat.
He asks how work goes,
And if they treat me well,
And I can only answer with my head bowed
While the crown on his shines.
Afterwards I work quieter than ever,
Hiding my thoughts in pastry and gravy,
Kneading dough strong enough to swallow
Old fears.

He comes every day to the courtyard.
A word here and there, always gentle,
An acknowledgment, never a demand
Hidden in silk and suggestions.
Once, he asks me where I come from,
And I tell him,
I don't know, Your Majesty.
It's easier to say than the truth,
Which stirs the flayed fibers of my heart

In warning:
Be careful,
Be vigilant always.

But I have my coat, my disguise, and surely
Our exchanges are nothing but
Ordinary duties of a future ruler–
Odd he should be so attentive, but
Still.
I don't mind the conversation.

I find the seasons change easily
And the rhythms of the castle soothe me,
And my work keeps me almost thoughtless
Until the day he isn't in the courtyard,
And something strange squeezes in my chest,
A notice of what I'd come to expect.
How can I miss someone who doesn't know me?
Inside, the kitchen buzzes.
A ball, they say, *and what a lot of cooking*
We've got to do! It's lucky
You're here to help.

I plait dough and bake tarts and ice cakes,
And my coat itches.
Has it grown tight these months,
Wearisome?
I think of the gowns I brought,
How soft they would feel,
How no one knows–
And strangely, as if I
Am someone else,
Or maybe some past version of myself,
That night I shed my stitched skin

And exhale,
Stepping into an old dress
That feels new.
Just one night.
I can put it back on afterwards,
And no one will know.

And no one does. The candlelight
Dazzles, the music brings tears to my eyes,
And the sight of the dancers
Makes me want to go back,
Back to the dark kitchen with its smells.
I turn and a voice says,
Leaving so soon?
Kind eyes regard me,
A gentle hand extends,
And I find I want to dance with him,
The prince,
Who surely does not know who I am.
Even I need not know.
Tonight, I invent myself again
In his arms, as the music
Swirls around us.

But the dancing ends and he
Wants to know my name,
Where I am from, and I
Must flee again,
Return to my coat of skins,
To anonymity,
To my dark little bed,
To forgetful sleep,
To another day in the kitchen.

The servants speculate on the strange princess
As we work.
I only smile.
I want him to be in the courtyard, but
He isn't.
Perhaps he has forgotten me,
And just as well.
I work my mind into silence
But my coat itches worse than ever.
When did it become so stiff?

The day stretches longer than ever until
Night,
And music,
And the servants leave and at last
I shed my coarse skin
For a gown of gold.

He dances with me again,
And nothing else matters.
He asks no questions,
And we dance many times,
And I embrace the fiction
As his arms encircle me.
I never want to leave.
I excuse myself at the ball's end,

Reluctantly,
And he releases me much the same way,
A word bitten back on his lips.

The next morning I am humming,
Bringing kitchen scraps to pigs

In the courtyard when he comes, and
My heart trips as he smiles.
He asks me if I like my work still,
If I get enough to eat,
And I answer *yes* with downcast eyes.
How does your majesty enjoy the ball?
He is silent as we walk, then,
There was a woman, he says, *someone remarkable,*
—My heart leaps—
A wise and kind princess, and her father the king
Did something terrible. She had no choice
But to leave.
I would have asked this king's blessing to marry her,
But
I have learned he is cruel, and besides I believe
She must be free to make her own choice.

I cannot walk.
I know he watches.
He waits.
He knows.
He knows.
My silly fiction was just that—
A lie, a fragile shell.
The silver threads jangle warning around my
Bruised heart:
Be ever vigilant.
I should not have stopped listening.
The coat was not enough.
He cannot want me—
I cannot let him—

I drop the bucket,
Flee the courtyard,
My coat of skins heavy and stinking of

Fear
Running until the trees swallow sight of
The castle turrets
And the forest embraces me again,
Running past the roots and nettles, where
Once abandoned parts of me raised timid eyes,
Running like a hare chased by hounds,
Hounds I will never outrun.
I return to the creature I was,
I am
Stained with the shame and the crime
And the silent cry.

Weary and senseless of time, I see white
Falling and covering the ground.
I sink down
And find myself near a broken wall,
Dusted with snow.
This wall—I sit up and look around.
I know this place.
It is the place I fled.
My steps have led me back.

I cannot escape.

Instead of leaving,
I stay.
I am tired of fleeing.
And this place, once grand,
Is small, reduced, crumbling.
No one stops me as I reach the doors
Treading with trembling legs that don't
Feel like my own.
I enter the castle, the hall, the rooms

Where servants flit like ghosts.
They are anxious, quiet, and
The stink of death is on the place.
Bile rises in my throat.

Shame and crime and silent cry

I forge my way down endless corridors,
Knowing backwards
Is the way ahead,
My coat a soothing weight
On my fearful body.
All these months I have stitched
Myself together,
And I will hold.
Let me hold.

At first he does not recognize me,
The king,
My father.
He lies pale and drawn on his bed.
Then his eyes widen and he cries out,
Says my name,
Chokes on his own voice,
His own shame, his own crime.
I am silent.
I am silent when he shudders and his body fails
And I am silent when his breathing stops.

Only when I drift back outside on
Trembling legs that feel terribly like my own,
Only when I reach the broken wall
Do I sob and scream and retch,

Expelling layers of pain and unnamed things
And horrors long asleep.
I am peeled raw, bleeding, old wounds weeping white.

Then I walk.

This place is not mine anymore.
The past, I abandon.
My heart is silent.
Peace or exhaustion, I cannot tell.
Surely peace would feel brighter.

I can make myself again wherever I
Decide to stay,
Turning my feet away from all
Previous paths.
Let these raw wounds heal,
Leave ugly scars like bad
Stitches,
Holding in all the tender parts that should never
Have been torn.
I tell myself this as I leave the forest behind—
No castle spires here, only villages.

I find work in a tavern where there is much to do.
If there is little kindness, there is no trouble, and I
Work hard.
There are cakes to make, roasts to watch, and
No one complains about my strange coat or
Asks me where I come from.

When flowers grow in window boxes and walkways,

Banners adorn the crooked streets, and
There is extra food to prepare. I do not ask
Why everyone is merry and expectant,
Why the villagers don their best clothes.
I myself have begun a new dress, a plain thing.
I complete tasks without question, willing my heart to
Stay silent.
But he is not.

We see each other in the back alley,
He, a prince, looking unprincely and so,
So like a word I must not say,
And tears fill his eyes.
Are you well? Do they treat you fairly?
I nod and go inside, and he does not follow
Even though a prince could go wherever he chooses,
Demand as he pleases.
There will be no ball, no gold dresses, no dancing.
My heart must be silent and not ask for anything.

He is there the second night, while merrymaking fills the
streets.
I linger and so does he, in silence, uncomplicated,
A moment of simplicity.
He is there the third night, and we speak of odd things.
My father is dead, I tell him. *I won't go back ever again.*
Did you mean what you said, about
My choice being my own?
Yes, he says.
Always your own.

The fourth night his visit is brief,
Only a word or two,
As people expect to see their prince.

My coat has begun to itch again.
The next day I finish sewing my new dress.
It is simple, replacing the rags beneath my
Coat of skins, but it stops the chafing.

The fifth night is his last.
I want so badly to ask him to hold me,
As he did when we danced.
But there are so many reasons I cannot.
I would ask a question of you, he says, *if I thought*
It would not send you running again.
Why did you not come after me? I ask.
Because you are no hind to chase or deer to stalk,
He says,
Because love is not a prison.

I am weeping and cold.
I don't know if I can...
I might never...
He says he knows.
I can't promise to be both
wife and lover.
He holds out his hand towards me. I
Put mine in his and the chill runs away.
You don't have to, says the prince.

What if I run again?

Then I will wait. You can always
Find me
When you are ready.

Ask me, then, I say, *ask me and I'll tell you.*

Somewhere on the journey home with my prince, I
Lost my coat of skins,
Fallen off like a scab no longer needed.
Sometimes I miss it.
It told a story
Of how I began to remake myself
With furs and flour, thread and mince pies.
But I wear my story on my skin
And this flesh is a tender dwelling.
My heart, still bruised, is mending.
I cannot say what new story we will make,
My love and I,
But if the way he looks at me is any indication,
By the way our joined hands feel like a mending
Of their own,
I believe it will be a good one.

Wild the Women - Beth Stedman

Lily of the valley,
beautiful and bright,
did you meet the devil
in the fading light?

Willow by the river,
weeping in your jail,
at the tainted crossroads,
made with him a deal.

Oak lift up your branches,
tall throughout the storm.
In the woods' sweet darkness
let him take you home.

Maiden, do you whisper
secrets of your own?

Mother, are you singing
down into the bone?

Crone, what can you tell me
of this harrowed life?

"Leave gardens for the forest
take with you–
a knife."

List of Fairy Tales, Folklore, and Myths

All Kinds of Fur (Germany): *Kitchen Magic, Stitches*

Beauty and the Beast (France): *Beauty, Beast, Belle's Delicious Library*

Bluebeard (France): *Bluebeard*

Cinderella (Germany): *By the Cinders, Hand-me-downs, Kitchen Magic*

The Frog Prince (Germany/United States): *Bayou Blues*

Iron Henry (Germany): *The Hoop Around My Heart*

Jorinde and Joringel (Germany) *Jorinde, The Bird Witch*

The Tale of the Bamboo Cutter (Japan): *Kaguya-Hime*

Little Mermaid (Denmark): *Displaced Mermaid, On the Surface, The Mermaid's Sacrifice*

Little Red Riding Hood (France/Germany): *Haiku of a Red Hooded Girl, Red and the Wolf*

Maid Maleen (Germany): *Three Women*

Peter Pan (England/United States): *Tink's Discovery*

The Arabian Knight (Near/Middle/Far East): *The Princess and the Cobbler*

Rapunzel (Germany): *Rapunzel's Rhapsody, Ropes & Reins*

The Mabinogion (Wales): *Rhiannon (The Lady of Yesterday)*

Rumpelstiltskin (Germany): *Rumpelstiltskin's Daughter*

Sleeping Beauty (France): *Maleficent's Lament, Vigil*

Snow White (Germany): *Snow Eats an Apple, Snow White*

Swan Lake (Russia/Germany): *Black Swan*

Twelve Dancing Princesses (Germany): *12 Cinquains for 12 Dancing Princesses, The Cloak of Invisibility*

White Bear King Valemon (Norway): *VALEMON*

Thank you

Stephanie Escobar:

To Harrison, my prince who rescues me from my tower over and over again. Our happily ever afters are recurring and endless.

To Ophelia, the princess who made me a queen. May you always believe in love and magic, but most importantly the love and magic abundant within yourself.

To my mother, who raised me with a heart of longing and eyes that seek out magic in the mundane.

To Stephanie, my name twin, editor and creator of this collection. You are one of the greatest fairytale weavers I've had the pleasure of knowing. You may be a gentle maiden, worthy of happily-ever-afters and sweet ballads, but you, my darling, are also a slayer of dragons. I admire you so.

Caitlin Gemmell:

To my fellow Fairy Tale Spinners, especially Stephanie for initiating this group project: I'm so grateful for connecting with you in our poetry salon. The magic we created is stronger because we worked on it together.

To my son Harry: thank you for inspiring me to be the best person I can be so I can bring magic into your life. I hope my words find their way to your heart one day.

To Justin: thank you for coming back into my life just when I needed a best friend most. You remind me of the person I was before circumstances broke me. You help to mend me. I love you, dear friend.

To my friends and family: thank you for encouraging me to follow my heart and chase after those things that bring me joy.

Cortney Joseph:

I first want to thank God for never allowing me to give up on myself or my dreams and talent. Had I done so, I'd have never gotten the chance to be part of such a wonderful project.

I want to thank my family for always believing in me and pushing me to keep going. Mine is one of the less conventional career paths and I'm so very glad to have such a wonderful support system behind me with each step and choice that I make.

I want to say thank you to all of the wonderful ladies included in The Wistful Wild for thinking of me and allowing me to contribute my words to such a fun collection. I'm so glad to have jumped back into writing, and to have done so with you all.

Jess Lynn:

Reading fairy tales as an adult feels a lot like getting free—shaking off the old and stepping into the power and strength that comes not only from storytelling, but the storytelling power of women. I am so grateful for the women who lead and dance and pursue their freedom in story and words, unafraid of the shadows. Your pursuit encourages me. This is a road toward healing and I'm glad to be walking it with you. And to Stephanie, a dancing woman, thank you for this opportunity to be part of these wistful and wild women.

To my children...thank you for humoring me and joining along for all the fairy and folk tales I make you listen to. If you ever get caught in the woods with Death, at least you'll know how to trick him. Thanks to my husband Joe, who held down the fort when I broke my back and was working through edits, but also for ignoring how many books on fairy tales I actually buy. I can only promise more.

Beth Stedman:

I'm eternally grateful to my Grandma Bear for giving me my first book of poetry. That book of classic poems sparked a love of poetry in me that continues to burn today. I have to also thank Ali Noël whose weekly #posttopoet poetry prompts inspired me to return to my own floundering attempts at writing poetry.

Thank you to my husband and two kids, who put up with my mad dashes from the dinner table to get down the elusive words that sprang up at the most inconvenient moments.

Thank you to Stephanie Ascough for reaching out with that first tentative ask and including me in this dream project of yours. And thank you to each of the lovely women who submitted poems to this collection. Your words inspire and humble me.

Stephanie Ascough:

To Ethan, Emmie, Kellan, and Brendan: for expanding my heart, imagination, and sleep deprivation. May the stories being written now make your future even richer.

To Mike: for listening to my writing rambles and rants, even when you have no idea what I'm talking about. Once upon a time, not so very long ago, I wore a coat of many furs. Life isn't a fairy tale, and sometimes it's the darkest kind, but even still you make me believe that just maybe we can have our happy ever after.

To Stephanie: for your unmatched encouragement and faith in me. Your kind words put me at a loss for words, and I couldn't ask for a better Name Twin.

To Caitlin: for your unique blend of gentleness and ferocity. For your own kind of magic that you bring everywhere you go, and which you share so creatively in so many ways.

To Cortney: for generously sharing your beautiful creations and beautiful self. I'm so glad we crossed paths through our Wordpress blogs a few years ago. It's been a joy getting to know you and your writing better.

To Jess: for reminding me that though we moms of four have our doubts & mountains of responsibilities, we're still humans full of dreams. For proving that we can still wander barefoot through the trees dressed in flowing gowns.

To Beth: for inspiring me with your bold and raw words. For going the extra mile and offering me sound editing advice. For all the juicy Marco Polo chats and insightful beta readings.

To all the Fairy Tale Spinners: thank you for joining me around the fire. Thank you for bringing your unique styles and perspectives to this book. Thank you for graciously handling my often-last-minute editing requests. Stirring the cauldron with you has been inspiring, fun, and life-giving.

Author Bios

Stephanie Escobar

Stephanie Escobar is the author of several short stories and the Gothic, ghostly romance, *A Song Beyond Walls*. She devotes her storytelling to the more lamentable, yearnful perspectives of women, mothers, and young girls, as a mother herself – especially, the mother of a daughter.

She resides in the Pacific Northwest, where she finds solace in the rainy woodlands with a steaming cup of espresso. When she isn't writing, she is either scouring antique shops for unique treasures (let's be honest, it's mainly for old books), baking all things able to be dunked in coffee, and searching for new and scenic outdoor adventures to embark upon with her family.

Stephanie welcomes visitors to her website (sescobarauthor.com) and encourages readers to connect with her on Goodreads.

Caitlin Gemmell

Caitlin Gemmell (she/her) is a poet and prose writer living in the countryside of upstate New York. She's the founder of #enchantedsimplicity and the author of *Spinning Hair Into Gold* (2019) and *True North* (2022). Her poems have been published in *Rue Scribe, One Sentence Poems, Minison Zine,* and the Autumn 2022 Anthology by Querencia Press.

Cortney Joseph

Born and raised in Baton Rouge, Louisiana, Cortney Joseph picked up her pen at the age of ten and hasn't set it down since. Finding inspiration in the pens of African-American authors and songwriters, she learned quickly that her stories could be told in more than the monolith she'd been presented in early childhood.

Deciding to share her work with the world, she self-published her first collection of poetry at the age of 21. Building an online audience since about 2012, she now runs MyPenWritesNice.com where she shares her poems, short stories, and more. An independent author; to date, Cortney has published 7 poetry collections and is eagerly sharing bits and pieces of her art with her online community.

Twitter : @MyPenWritesNice
Instagram : @MyPenWritesNice

Jess Lynn

Jess Lynn is a lover of stories, wearer of flower crowns, and still believes in magic and wonder. She writes for the girl who never grew up and for the one wondering if hope is a joke (she's been there too). She finds inspiration in the truth that every thing, every person, every happenstance and history has its own story. She sees her work as an intersection of history, myth, and magic.

When her head's not stuck in a book or following rabbit trails of possible plot lines, she's busy building a life with her husband, mothering and home educating their four children (7 - 14), and ever so slowly renovating their 1917 farmhouse in South Carolina.

Beth Stedman

Beth Stedman lives in Phoenix, AZ, with her husband and two kids.
She writes kissing books with magic and co-hosts Fable & The
Verbivore, a podcast for writers who read and readers who write.
When she isn't writing her own stories, she's working as a book
coach and helping authors write books readers can't put down. She
loves staying up all night reading "one more chapter" and eating
more chocolate than is healthy for any one human to consume.

You can connect with her and find writing tips, book reviews,
updates on her projects, and ridiculous reels on her
Instagram: @bethstedman

Stephanie Ascough

Stephanie Ascough (she/her) is a neurodivergent writer who loves folklore and fairy tales. She has published two books: *A Land of Light and Shadow*, a middle grade fantasy, and *Flower and Cloak*, a collection of short fairy tales, as well as poems and short stories in other publications.

When she isn't writing or researching her latest special interest, you can find her reading, avoiding housework, or exploring the Appalachian Mountains of Tennessee, where she lives with her husband, four children, and cat/fae. Connect with her on Instagram @author.stephanieascough, or through her newsletter, The Purple Vale, on Substack (purplevale.substack.com).

Lightning Source UK Ltd.
Milton Keynes UK
UKHW040722020223
416362UK00004B/309